I0671096

rhapsody 2014

an anthology of guelph writing

Vocamus Press
Guelph, Ontario

Published by Vocamus Press
©All rights reserved

Cover image by Ivano Stocco
©All rights reserved

ISBN 13: 978-1-928171-01-0 (pbk)
ISBN 13: 978-1-928171-02-7 (ebk)

Vocamus Press
130 Dublin Street, North
Guelph, Ontario, Canada
N1H 4N4

www.vocamus.net

2014

Preface

The Rhapsody Anthology is an annual collection of poetry and very short prose by writers who live in and around the city of Guelph, Ontario. It is a celebration of local writing that includes both authors who are well established in their craft and those who are published here for the first time, reflecting the variety of writers and writing that formed the literary communities of Guelph during the year 2013 / 2014. The pieces are arranged simply in the order that they were posted on www.vocamus.net throughout the year.

The cover art was provided by Ivano Stocco. The cover and interior were designed by Jeremy Luke Hill.

Acknowledgements

Thanks to all the contributors for sharing their work so generously. Special thanks to Ivan Stocco for allowing his art to be used for the book cover. Thanks finally to all those who contribute to the literary culture of Guelph as readers, writers, publishers, sponsors, venues, broadcasters, and in countless other ways – this collection is a celebration of all that you do.

rhapsody

2014

an anthology of guelph writing

CONTENTS

Guelph Elect Lights   1
Shane Neilson

Concession Stand   3
Burl Levine

Anxious, and the Climate Differs   5
Joel McNutt

Travelling Against   9
Karen Houle

The Spit   11
Michael Kleiza

Not For Lack of Love or Want   13
Andrew Hood

Bell Curve   15
Madhur Anand

Consider the Idea of Good Enough   17
Claire Tacon

No Farewell   19
Bieke Stengos

taking vows   21
valerie senyk

Polio   23
Nicholas Ruddock

I am running   25
Carrie Snyder

The Friends   27
Rob O'Flanagan

Dead Bugs   31
Jerry Prager

This Is Changing   33
Amelia (Meme) Meister

Order   35
Douglas Davey

I'm Out   39
Kai van der Meer

The Settler   41
Cid Brunet

Courting Lightness   43
Michelle McMillan

A Time That No One Reads   45
Jeremy Luke Hill

If Love   47
Nikki Everts-Hammond

The Plough   49
Matt Payne

Prison   51
Darcy Hiltz

Guelph Elect Lights
Shane Neilson

Elect lights elegize the downtown.
With ill-fitting skates, my son is held
by his mother. He prefers to flop, gather snow
to his mouth, to look at her as I've long looked:
the beginning and end of a full breath.

First made in budget meetings, the ice was predicted
by closed roads cursed under modest spires.
In the shadow of the Co-Operators rooftop,
boyfriends and girlfriends make circles of ice
as the Ackers Furniture sign aches for paint.

I've walked the streets of my own Bethlehem
and looked into shop windows as if on sale
were a life I'd want to live again. I see men
and women only, but I need to see. In the degree
of freedom that is mad, men look for the sure.

A church bell rings. The sun slips past old eaves.
Light drops to make Guelph Music lose the austere
glitter of guitar rock. A homeless man shouts
from the end of Carden while kids push plastic chairs
for balance and our lovers retrace.

Message on a concrete ledge: In Loving Memory
of Nicholas Lambden. I often sit with my son and feel
as if I am looking at a house with no windows or glass.
The Nicholas who died is the provenance of a park
in the heart of a city with modest schools, small hospitals,
a university – enough to sate citizen kings.

1

My son takes his first strides toward the ledge.
He climbs, dangles his legs, bangs his blades.
He looks past the overhang of street level shops
and second-floor lofts, to sky. Like me, he seeks.

Around his mouth is melted snow. Love for display –
Guelph's dead make for an otherwise joy? For me:
a boy, a woman, all that can't live, the evidence of all
that does, Lambden Square stunned by domestic
grief, yet: see the lighted faces and covet this city.

Concession Stand
Burl Levine

whenever the occasion arises
that the Canadian Senate is to
commence being in session,
this leading repository of rogues
should unanimously stand in unison
and concede to the anonymous electorate
that being deliberately vague
is no longer in vogue

indeed, and in deed,
the cursory whispers and whimpers
that reverberate reprehensibly
within these rank corridors of corruption
have turned this formerly revered
haven of hope into a hypocritically
hollow, no longer hallowed,
speakeasy for lispers

Anxious, and the Climate Differs
Joel McNutt

Day one:

Transforming your you to recognize you're you
and alone
in space, with a fifteen foot ceiling,
     and a narrow winding staircase–
        to bed, to climb, to sleep.

Transforming your you in a room without light or a door,
and where the grey carpeting will never
find its place in history,
     remains ignored and forgotten:
        a struggle for words, not inspiration–
making mid-day
     the best time
        to sleep.

...and I'm still afraid the General's coming for me.

Anxious, and the climate differs

Day two:

Transforming the you, with some comfort and control,
     to I,
        to confront, with that comfort and control–
somewhere between the toilet running every half the hour,
     the me.
So it's not shivering on one side,
     and sweating the other.

Transforming the you in a space above the nicest carpet,
    which is torn
        fifteen feet above the lowest floor,
between company,
    and the same old settled routines.
No one will argue
    lime green
        has its place
            in history.

...and I've been meaning to ask the nurse if my legs could have a
    fever.

Anxious, and the climate differs

Day three:

and the cure was simple

Anxious with my body, but longing to show
"I want you to see me naked," said to her
And so, I stepped back into myself.

I
stood erect, naked,
facing a soon-to-be lover.

From where she lay, nestled beneath the blankets
freshly made for the first time in weeks.
For her:
    I even washed the pillow case that hugs her cheeks.

I knew there wasn't the company of shadows through the window
    that framed me,

to hide from view, skin parts or curves.
Just me, all of me:
      naked,
            erect,
                  and exposed, to her.

Pale and tender,
I felt that night, on what seemed the longest night,
that I fit myself rather nicely.

And I did; I could sense acceptance in her stare.
In the call for bareness a body seduces,
as if it's summertime,
the first time,
a body's been naked.

I felt awkward only for a moment–
About the amount of time it takes to pull an old glove from your
        pocket
And slide it over your hand
on a cool, November morning.

Written across the palm must've read:

"This is me, all of me, the I, the you.
See me, study me.
This is me: erect, naked, pale, and tender."

...because I finally knew:
        all of me
            fits well
                with all of you.

Anxious, and the climate differs.

Travelling Against
Karen Houle

Give me the common or the rare, as they roll

We are mistaken in what we survive,
in what we must eliminate.

The ladies at the plate glass persist,
reviving their brutal martyrdoms,
worn thin by the abuse of soap,
the contour of teacups in unison

against smallpox, cosmetic agriculture,
and wartime rape. And a woman

they believe unrecognizable
as such.

She is given to volatility around faith.
Faith in where the unlivable gathers

like thistle,
like wild yeast's affinity for chance

where sexual impatience bursts from the sudden rise
like malady. And it is knee-deep

in mustard, in scattered hybrids
of deliberate imperfection.

Slice through against chronicle. Slip your thumb
under the seam where the signal tugs
forward. Pain,

where you grasp it,
is not what you don't want
any more

than an uncontaminated vat remains sterile,
and cannot

Be treated better,
Or promoted across palate.

Be perverse in your indifference to recommend
a local history. Keep the virus for study,
keep this loss of mime. I know

so little,

my arts are often mistaken
in their assemblies, their lambic filiations
among grain and tool. But

it is such hands
as mutate all along the breed,

And travelling against,
And loud.

* Previously published in *Ballast* (House of Anansi Press, 2000)

The Spit
Michael Kleiza

We pick our way over the crushed tongue
of stacked concrete and rusted rebar where
children imagine ribs
of a Tyrannosaur and screech
in chorus with the gulls.

Garbage bags jammed in the rocks
snap premonitions in a wind
that breathes only cold
on my neck.

I sit as a boy combs
the shoreline, picking through the jetsam
of scattered glass that shines like coloured suns
in the damp gravel.
Desperate to please, he runs to me;
fills my cupped hand with emerald,
lapis and ruby. I plunder
his wide-eyed age.

Not For Lack of Love or Want
Andrew Hood

Before the baby there were things to learn, shit to get deft at and master.

"Buying stuff is not the same as doing stuff or learning stuff," the girl he loved who he'd babied-up said. "Remember."

At the guitar shop he demurred over banjos, figuring furrowed indecision would pass for knowledge. In the end, he bought the third most expensive. "I'd get the Gibson," he assured the clerk, "but there's a baby on the way."

At home he put a finger pick on each finger, made cat claws.

"I think that's too many picks," the girl with the baby in her said.

"We'll see," he said, as he tried to figure out what was wrong with the internet so he could get on and prove her wrong.

Over the months, he ruined two good pots trying to make chocolate, cut off the tip of his finger buzzing wood for the crib, and his left arm still smarted sometimes from the shock he got putting another light in the nursery.

After the baby came out of the girl's body, he didn't like holding it. Not for lack of love or want, but a certainty that he would drop and kill the thing.

Bell Curve
Madhur Anand

We are learning how to divide gulls: pinkness of leg,
thickness of beak, herring or ring-billed. The naked eye
can't tell from a distance. True things, even the matter
-of-factness of a seabird cry, have a tendency
to fly. Fine lines, first v-shaped then imperceptible
on the horizon. We may slow down, domesticate,
adjust our binoculars, memorize the guidebooks
move out to the coast, yet still not stop the new truths: White
-eyed, black-backed, yellow-footed, brown-hooded,
      glaucous-winged,
swallow-tailed. We take this course, and I think we all get
the credit. See, it's the common that dictates the wild
undercurrents of interior, surface, or sea.

* A previous version of this poem was published in *Contemporary Verse 2* (2010)

Consider the Idea of Good Enough
Claire Tacon

The dentist was busy trying to fit a dental dam into Derek's mouth. The perforated holes for his molars didn't line up, and the rubber kept snapping out of the dentist's latex gloves. The frame holding the dam in place had hit Derek twice. The dentist hadn't apologized. Derek had hoped for some acknowledgment, running his tongue pointedly over the abused tooth.

"Bet you'll be flossing every night after this," the dentist chuckled.

That wasn't the solution Derek had arrived at. But he did feel nostalgia for those missed opportunities. Suck candies paraded in front of him, like orthodontic ghosts of Christmas Past. He'd eaten bins of them in the past six months since his sister had died of cancer and he'd given up smoking. Not that he was about to explain that to this glad-hand with a drill. The X-rays had revealed five cavities. Five, after twenty-seven years without one. He'd smoked since he was fifteen and everyone said it would ruin his teeth. But not smoking, apparently, was worse. He'd have to switch to something else, sugar-free. But weren't those chemicals bad too? Weren't they worming through his tissue, carving pathways for disease just the same?

"My sister was a runner," he said when the dentist released his mouth to reach for an implement.

"Sorry?"

"Runner, organic food. House in the country. Good air. Died of a massive stroke a few months ago."

"I'm so sorry."

"I floss every day. Usually twice. Take my toothbrush to the office to get a lunchtime rub in."

"I didn't mean to imply."

"When your number's up."

The dentist nodded, calm and serious. Dropped his dental mask to show his respect.

Of course, it wasn't true. She'd smoked more than him, ate processed foods, had a stationary bike that collected more dust than miles. But she still didn't deserve that slow decline, that terrible wasting.

And he didn't deserve to sit here and be lectured by a dentist who couldn't handle his own instruments. Ten to one, the hygienist could have accomplished the task by now. If you can fix it, he thought, why the hell do you need to assign blame?

No Farewell
Bieke Stengos

Once upon a life
I sailed from Kiparissia
its craggy mountaintops
like thorns
in my bleeding heart
the waves of the sea
beckoning me
with their incessant slaps
against the prow
of my little boat

Sixteen I was
a girl still
but yet a woman
under the hot
greedy hands
of Michaelis
a cousin twice removed
on my mother's side
who taught me
where love pulses
in the heat of my belly

A girl I was
and he a man
whose eager breath
awakened flames
in my soft wet flesh
whose wanting mouth
opened gaping wounds

upon my pulsing throat
until my mother found us
and ordered me
to go and live
the dry life of repentance
in far away America

From Kiparissia I sailed
with tears as salt
as the moving sea
and Michaelis
receding on the shore
His red kerchief
in my flailing hand
was torn by the wind
and landed
upon the dark waters
where it stayed and swayed
refusing to bid
a last adieu

* This poem was the winner of the BC Hope Writer's Guild Poetry Contest

taking vows
valerie senyk

we never spoke about the shape of things
that was left to chance, imagination, heredity

the road ahead was as littered as a winter beach
sadder because, in its twists and turns, no guideposts

the animals that crouched in our minds stood at the ready
the circus we created was as multi-ringed as DNA

we didn't know a thing beyond a snarled profusion of yarn
and not knowing was the only place to begin

Polio
Nicholas Ruddock

In 1953 the polio virus hovered over the summertime streets of Toronto, it multiplied in the warmth of slow-moving creeks and in the shallow sands of Ward's Island, in rainfall it slipped down from the canopy of maple, elm, heat and cicadas, vaporizing into random bedrooms thought secure, tasteless on the tongues of those who lay commingled there. Over breakfast we heard radio accounts of children slumped like rags, breathless, cyanotic, living out their lives within relentless metal carapaces, "iron lungs" pushing, pulling at the paralyzed chest itself incapable of moving air, and those children who had been rendered voiceless by tracheotomy used their teeth to go click-click-click drawing the attention of nurses to their plight (real or imagined) and the click-click-clicking ratcheted up as the sky darkened with ozone and thunder and the threat of power failure which would bring parents, neighbours and passers-by unimpeded to the open wards in a rush of fear-of-smothering, the starch white dresses of the nurses "like moths" amidst the to-and-fro swishing of tubes, the children lying as though beheaded, the sick quarantined, the healthy (you and I) taken to the cedar-filled air of Inverhuron where the second of the Great Lakes beat against a series of reefs straight out from shore, where in the last shelf of rock (before the lake dropped off to what seemed to us to be fathoms of darkness) we could see the petrified coral bodies of tiny crustaceans, locked into their airless world centuries before polio.

I am running

Carrie Snyder

I am in Waterloo Park and I am running

the path slick with mud
dry with sun
barren with autumn's undoing
patched with ice

and I am running

ducks and deer crowd and part
picnic blankets snap flat
children in green pursue a ball
a loose dog a peacock's rasp
swings rise and fall in rhythmic peace
a bicycle's bell, winding secret trails
sweet boredom argued promises
sweeter repose

and I am running

boardwalk embrace–does she love him?–does he
love her?–what will endure?

cross-legged solitary on a stone
family frozen for the camera
steady rearrangement of picnic tables
shoreline recedes schoolhouse stands silent
a cricket match a shout
a season's sharp turn

soccer on snow
bitter January surprised by
impromptu joy and unzipped parkas

ring of pavement cresting steep

I am running
I am running

who remembers once upon a time
there was a bear, caged, here?

The Friends

Rob O'Flanagan

I

I came apart in the park today.
First, a leg wobbled and fell off,
then a hand flapped in the wind
and set sail like paper to the sky.
My proud chin detached, fell to the
ground and was spirited away by a bird.
My heart was lost in the high grasses.

In pieces, the friend found me
on one knee, undone.
We talked of ordinary things:
the artistry of birds in flight,
the grace of God to find us when
shattered.

Together, we searched
the high grasses.

II

I am lonely for my disappeared ones,
for the friends vanished into the thin air of life.

When time and space separates the friends,
we call to one another in our souls and answer
through thin air, crying out wordlessly,
communicating in the depths.

And when we are together again, in groups
in homes, our eyes acknowledge the boundless
conversation our spirits have had,
and we embrace and speak our love.

III

Can you have me over?
I am no big trouble.
Any form of hot beverage
will suffice to loosen my tongue
to laud the name of my friend.
But only if he melts away my reserve
and consents to be spoken of.

IV

I tried to push out the wings all day,
barely taking time to breathe.

It is an effort to learn how to fly,
to push out what you know to be
just under the surface.

A friend came and sat with me
and told me of an article she had read
about wings imprinted in stone and the
evolution of flight.
"It has taken so long for birds to learn
their tricks," she said.

I stopped pushing
and took a breather.

She asked how it felt,
now that I was
light enough to fly.

V

One should never say too much
over the broadcast system
when they are lonesome
or hungry for love

when tests weigh me down
a stranger inhabits my throat
and never says anything worth
hearing.

I am told some grace in the
form of a friend will eventually come
with song, bread or drink
to help me find my voice again.

I am told to remember that
all cold and gloom passes
when the friend finds you
huddled and tongue tied.

Remember what love and
joy sound like when vibrating
in your throat.

Dead Bugs
Jerry Prager

There are dead bugs in my bed, live ones on my wall:
they come every year, little blue gray bugs, with wings,
although I've never seen them fly. I went to visit my
ex-girlfriend and one fell out of my suit. They have
a graveyard in my window sill that I vacuum up now and then;
that must be hell for them.

This Is Changing

Amelia (Meme) Meister

The newness of your breath in my ear
Was enough to forget oceans
I hid in a valley and watched us climb
No travellers cared
To question two lovers without
water bottles or tents to last the night

Mountains seemed insignificant
In the sight of new love

I cannot travel anymore
Like this
My mouth is parched for wanting
My clothes tattered from hope

How do we descend together
And not reach the underworld?
For I do not want death to haunt our bedside
But winds to scatter the seeds that we have
Nurtured within the fruits of our love
To grow into a field that we can lay in
Without staring at clouds that fly by
Like dreamscapes

Order
Douglas Davey

They showed him the list DOG CAT HORSE COW MOUSE SHEEP and told him to put the list in alphabetical order so he did AC-CDEEEEGHHMOOOOPRSSSTUW but then they told him that no they wanted each *word* in alphabetical order. Even cow? Yes, of course even cow. So he sorted the list again DGO ACT EHORS COW EMOSU EEHPS and then they said I'm sorry can you put the *words* in order yes he could but no he did not want to.

He was tired. These were not good games they were bad games that made things come apart and so he pushed the list away and sat on the rug which was a map and he tapped the world together again:

Tap

Tap tap tap

Tap tap tap tap tap

Tap tap tap tap tap tap tap

Tap tap tap tap tap tap tap tap tap tap tap

And on and on until thirty-seven when the numbers went down again.

Was he ready to play a different game no he was not. There was too much that was all around him a light that hummed and a strange smell. Things were all pulled apart in ways that were wrong and needed to be put together again with the right kind of pattern and sound *mmm mmm mmm* for radii made from red blocks around a center point C which was also was the perfect center of the room. Then coughing noises *hng hng, cng cng* for blue and green blocks that made a pattern across the rug which was a map. Why aren't you making a pattern now I *am* making a pattern even if the two ladies who made night bug noises can't see it. One of them had blue shoes and one blue shoe pushed a block out of place and he had to replace it or else all of his holding together wouldn't work.

The one without the blue shoes said would he like to return to the table and sit down? She touched his back and it was bad like cotton balls and he didn't like it but yes he would return to the table and sit down because things were held together.

Would he like more apple juice yes he would.

Could he sort these yes but how the star has five points and ten edges and a pentagon also has five points but also five edges which means it has the same number of points and edges like an octagon. Just sort them the way you think they should be sorted how can I sort them when I don't know how they are supposed to be sorted this game is bad.

One

Eight

Twenty-seven

Sixty-four

One hundred and twenty-five

Two hundred and sixteen

Three hundred and forty-three

Would he like to get off the floor and come back to his chair no he wanted to go to sleep. Please come back to your chair now.

They showed him a picture. What is happening in this picture the girl is standing up and the boy is lying down. Is anything wrong with the picture yes one of the girl's eyelids is a tangent. No is she behaving the way she should or is she doing something wrong she is just standing and the boy is just lying down. How do you know she is a girl because her hair is long. If a boy had long hair would he be a girl no he would not be a girl he would just be a boy with long hair.

Why is the boy sad I don't know. Was he hurt maybe he is asleep. He is crying maybe he is crying and asleep. Did the girl hurt him I don't know.

Things were coming apart again. He had to keep the whole world together and he was so tired. He sat on the rug and tapped everything back into place

Tap
Tap tap tap
Tap tap tap tap tap
And on and on until sixty-one. He took apart the pattern of red blocks and put it back in place with the center point *C* in the perfect center of the room.

I'm Out

Kai van der Meer

Then the snow fell deeply
whiting out the details
parking street signs shops
garden yards and walks–
all unlocked and lost.
The sun then shone along it
setting, the endless meadow
of wind brown grass of snow,
lighting golden roads to wild,
and I never came home.

The Settler
Cid Brunet

Ice will lid the river monster. A fish
in each hand to pacify the settler
who reclines, smoking, on burlap packed with salt.
With pelts and wealth, ambitions rise.
All evidence is in the blood spot.
Pilgrim; your teeth are parasite white.

Full moon crows moon bone white.
Wriggling into cold mud, lowly fish
know a harvest moon. They can spot
smoke rings blown into the stars by the settler.
He cleans his rifle. Slow to rise
heavy with gout, hard cheese and salt.

The hung carcass will need to be salt
rubbed to protect the meat from white
maggots who pool, spill, and rise.
Attacking unfortunate flesh like piranha fish.
Devastating sliver moons. Not unlike settler
families; swarming and breeding to claim a spot

which cannot be claimed. A black mold spot
growing. Sewing the soil with salt.
God granted him dominion with title; settler.
He brought his empty children. Just a white
skull where a face should be. Clammy fish
bellied palms rushing like a river on the rise

to colonize tributaries. The bleeding sunrise
transcended by an electric generation. Rare to spot
a golden birch or pick a morel. To glimpse a fish,
or witness a grizzly not taxidermied with salt
and sawdust. The sardonic museum sign, white,
described majesty to the children of the settler.

Unconvinced by facsimiles, the children of the settler
giggled at nature's oafish representation. Gave rise
to a creeping shame. Why would the white
tailed deer be reminiscent of grandfather's cancer spot?
A boring ghost with spit encrusted lips like sea salt.
Yet, at the exit, the children overlooked a prophetic fish;

Do not dream of us fish, you youthful settler.
Your blood is mostly salt. My fins cannot rise
from the grave spot you left me in; baking and white.

Courting Lightness
Michelle McMillan

Dense as the soles of his boots.
Fluid as plate glass.
He hides in his shadow,
Pressing hard temper on bone
In bursts of desire for softness.

He does not open his heart to the earth.
He does not trust the gravity of love.
He does not look up when the light changes
For fear of losing his place.
He does not dance when the mood changes
For fear of falling into her and losing control.

He looks back,
Resentful that his passion
Has made no impression on her.
Yet she will not let him leave
And the friction between them
Builds calluses that deaden feeling.

He dreams of leaping
Into the empty arms of the sky,
Rigid integrity stretched
Translucent against the sun.
Strength in the hollow of his bones.
Soaring with grace.

Seductive as an old textbook.
Brilliant as promise.
He hovers in his faith,
Courting lightness like a bird,
Breathless between landings.

A Time That No One Reads

Jeremy Luke Hill

The shadow-cool is longer than it was,
cast not just by a wan and sinking sun,
but by the passing of time, by all that time,
since a short shade was planted in memory
of something all but unremembered now,
so there is only shade, its sundial-sweep
through days, its creeping fingers in the grass,
to mark a time that no one ever reads,
that no one could hope to read, not by sight,
only by walking that slow sundial shade,
shadow-cool, always longer than it was.

If Love
Nikki Everts-Hammond

If love was an open door
I'd stand to one side
And let you go through first.

If love was a book
I'd find the page you were on
And thumb-down the corner.

If love was a virus
I'd hope it would infect you
Then I'd stand real close so it'd infect me too.

If love was a war
I'd fight on the other side
And try to meet you in battle.

If love was a tree
I'd warn it about the Chinook, but it wouldn't listen to me
Then I'd cry to see the tender, new leaves – frozen.

If love was darkness
I'd weave it into a cloak
And give it to you as a birthday present.

If love was a beggar on the street
I'd give him your best boots and a peanut butter sandwich
Then I'd walk with him to the ends of the earth.

The Plough
Matt Payne

The snow was devastating as I made my way downtown. I had to conjure up all my motivation for each thick footstep in the knee-deep snow. I should have taken the bus, but I hate taking the bus. It should only take twenty minutes to walk downtown, but this felt like hours. Had I already walked by that building? Old gray stone like many of this city's old buildings. In the dark they all looked the same.

I looked around again for Ron. Ron was still gone. We'd departed together. When did I lose him? It was dark enough that he could be close by and I wouldn't see him through the heavy snowfall. Snow should be white but in this darkness it was gray. I called out, "Ron!" But even if my feeble voice had escaped the scarf around my mouth, it would be drowned by the snow-plough behind me, scraping steadily along like a monster.

I was sure I'd passed by this church before, but I was also sure that I hadn't turned any corners. So it must be a different church. Lots of heritage in this city.

I couldn't walk on the sidewalks because they were dominated by a snowbank like a mountain range, with peaks and troughs by no pass through which to escape the road. All I could see was what the lamplights illuminated, and all of that was covered in snow. My knees were so tired, so tired of walking. This felt like a commercial for depression. I actually felt like giving up, but that plough behind me might not see me.

Had I passed that building already?

Where was Ron?

My ass muscles hurt from lifting my legs. My jeans were soaked right through. I wished I'd worn snowpants. I wished I'd taken the bus. The lamps all looked the same. They say every snowflake is unique, but they all looked the same to me. Peaceful little snowflakes falling from the heavens, working together to crush my spirit.

49

Deep down I knew that it shouldn't take so long to get downtown, even in this snow, but what else could I do? The effort of pushing forward, step by step by step, was already devouring my motivation. I couldn't think of these higher problems. These identical buildings. These hours and hours and hours... It was darkness all ahead, decorated with streetlights and snowflakes and the promise of difficult footsteps.

And that snow-plough. It seemed to be gaining on me.

Prison

Darcy Hiltz

row by row
Forbes, Shorts
Blacks and Humes
your stones weathered
all face one direction
like soldiers
at attention
a kind of unity
collective final act
by those who love you
some of you
are side by side
almost touching
bound by marriage
or blood
but the results are the same
you're held down
by dirt
confined behind
a metal fence
as if you might
leave to join
the living

www.ingramcontent.com/pod-product-compliance
Lightning Source LLC
Chambersburg PA
CBHW031902170626
46807CB00004B/1854